MW01121656

A WEEKEND IN THE CITY

LEE LORENZ

Pippin Press
New York

For Daphne and Chlöe

Published by Pippin Press, 229 East 85th Street, Gracie Station Box 92, New York, N.Y. 10028

Printed in the United States of America by Horowitz/Rae Book Manufacturers, Inc.

10 9 8 7 6 5 4 3 2 1

Library of Congress Cataloging-in-Publication Data

Lorenz, Lee.
A weekend in the city
Summary: As Pig and Duck describe to Moose the activities that they've planned for his visit to the city, Moose is reminded of similar but much more outrageous experiences he's had in the country.
[1. Animals—Fiction. 2. City and town life—Fiction. 3. Country life—Fiction. 4. Humorous stories.] I. Title.
PZ7.L884 1991
[E]—dc20 91-17153
ISBN 0-945912-15-3 CIP

"Next Saturday is Moose's birthday," said Duck.

"Let's send him a big chocolate cake," said Pig, "with marshmallow icing."

"I have a better idea," said Duck. "Let's invite him for a visit and throw him a surprise birthday party!"

"Great," said Pig. "Then we can *all* have some cake."

Duck went to the phone and called Moose.

"A weekend in the city? I'd sure like to see you boys, but is there anything to do down there?" asked Moose.

"Anything to do!" cried Duck. "There is *everything* to do. Tall buildings, fancy restaurants, great shows, museums... and you should see the new domed stadium. We can go to a baseball game there!"

"Get your ice cream, peanuts, ice-cold soda," added Pig.

"I used to love baseball," said Moose. "When I was younger I would practice pitching by painting a bullseye on the side of the barn. My fastball was so good I used to knock holes in the barn walls."

"Wow!" said Duck and Pig together.

"And," added Moose, "to protect the barn animals we had to move them into the house and up to the attic."

"Besides being a great pitcher, I was a terrific home-run hitter," Moose said.

"I would have turned pro, but I couldn't get a batting helmet on over my antlers. I can't watch a game now without feeling sad about that."

“We don’t want to make you feel sad,” said Duck.

“How about visiting the new Turbo Tower skyscraper?” asked Pig.

“You can see five states from there,” added Duck.

"There's a revolving restaurant on top," said Pig. "They serve just about every kind of food you can think of and they have a dessert bar with 34 different flavors of ice cream."

"Sounds pretty good," said Moose, "but I bet it can't beat what we used to get at the county fair. People still talk about my Aunt Myrna's sweet-potato ice cream."

"And I'll never forget the year Uncle Waldo's hot-pickled brussels sprouts exploded and burned down the tent."

“They had fire engines from six towns,” said Moose.

"It took them all day to put out the fire and nothing has grown in that field since."

"I guess a revolving restaurant doesn't sound like fun to you," said Duck. "Maybe you'd enjoy a parade instead. There's a big one next Saturday."

"There will be marching bands, floats, balloons, and flags waving," said Duck.

"And cotton candy, popcorn, and crackerjacks," added Pig.

"I *do* love parades, and especially the bands," said Moose. "In fact, I was the star tuba player in the Mooseville Marching Band. We had some great times!"

"I remember marching one day" Moose continued, "when a strong wind caught the tuba section and blew us clear into the next county."

"We landed right in the middle of a band contest," said Moose.

"We won first prize. I still have the trophies up in the attic."

“I guess our parade wouldn’t seem very exciting to you,” said Duck.

“How about the Space Museum?” said Pig. “They have a great cafeteria.”

"Space museum?" asked Moose.

"You know," said Duck, "they have a big telescope and a star show."

"They even have moon rocks," added Pig.

"Let me tell *you* about moon rocks," said Moose. "My Uncle Melvin had a telescope and he used to let me look through it sometimes."

"One night while I was watching the stars a flying saucer landed right next to me."

"Wow!" said Pig and Duck.

"Yes!" said Moose. "Some weird creatures took me for a ride all over the universe.

When they got back here they gave me a whole bucket of rocks from everywhere—the Moon, Mars, Venus!"

"I still use one to keep the barn door open," Moose added.

"Well, I give up," said Pig. "I guess there just isn't anything here to make your trip worthwhile."

"Now hold on a minute," said Moose. "I just happen to have a birthday next weekend and I can't think of anyone else I'd rather celebrate it with."

"Hooray!" shouted Duck and Pig together.
"You can take the 8:30 train," said Duck, "and we'll..."